Sleepover Squad

#3 The Trouble With Brothers

Grab your pillow and join the

SLEEPOVER SQUAD!

#1 *Sleeping Over*

#2 *Camping Out*

#3 *The Trouble with Brothers*

COMING SOON:

#4 *Whisper down the Lane*

P. J. DENTON

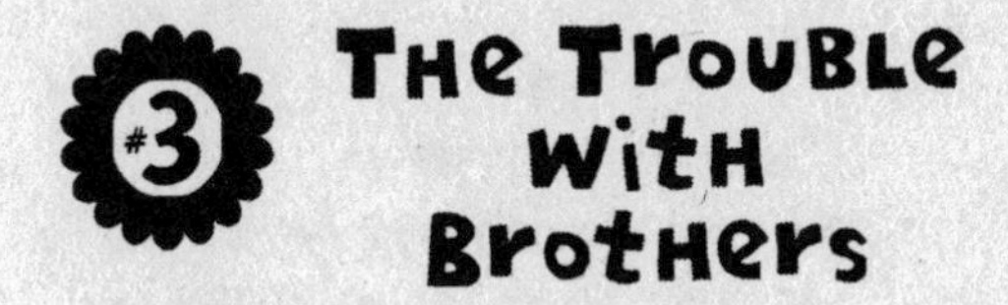

#3 The Trouble with Brothers

Illustrated by Julia Denos

ALADDIN PAPERBACKS
NEW YORK LONDON TORONTO SYDNEY

This book is a work of fiction. Any references to historical events, real people, or real locales are used fictitiously. Other names, characters, places, and incidents are the product of the author's imagination, and any resemblance to actual events or locales or persons, living or dead, is entirely coincidental.

ALADDIN PAPERBACKS
An imprint of Simon & Schuster Children's Publishing Division
1230 Avenue of the Americas, New York, NY 10020

Designed by Karin Paprocki
The text of this book was set in Cochin.
Manufactured in the United States of America
First Aladdin Paperbacks edition September 2007
2 4 6 8 10 9 7 5 3 1
Library of Congress Control Number 2006930151
ISBN-13: 978-1-4169-2800-3
ISBN-10: 1-4169-2800-6

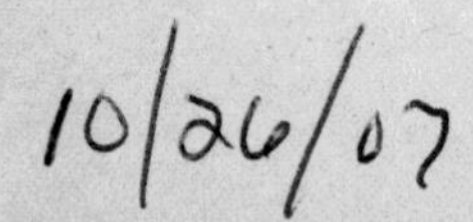

Sleepover Squad

#3 The Trouble with Brothers

1

Kara's Turn

"I love ice cream!" Kara Wyatt said with a happy sigh. She gazed at the double-chocolate cone in her hand, trying to decide which side to lick first.

Kara was sitting on a bench outside the ice-cream parlor. Two of her best friends, Emily McDougal and Jo Sanchez, were sitting beside her. Their other best friend, Taylor Kent, was hopping back and forth over a crack in the sidewalk. Taylor wasn't very good at sitting still.

"We heard you the first nine times you said that, Kara," Taylor teased. She hopped over the sidewalk crack again. Then she took a big bite from her maple-walnut cone.

Emily licked strawberry ice cream off her lips. "That's okay," she said. "I agreed with her all nine times. And I agree again."

"That means you agreed with her ten times," Jo said. Jo liked to be exact.

Kara took a big slurp of her ice cream. It tasted great, but it made her shiver a little. It was a crisp autumn afternoon, and the air felt cool even though the sun was shining.

A sudden breeze rattled the leaves of the big maple trees lining the street. It also blew a few strands of Kara's springy red hair across her face. The hair almost got into her ice cream, but Kara moved her cone away just in time.

"Brr." Jo was holding back her shoulder-length dark hair with one hand. "Pretty soon it will be too cold to eat ice cream anymore."

"No way!" Kara cried. "It's never too cold to eat ice cream."

"But it *will* be too cold to eat it outside." Taylor wrinkled her nose and looked down at the long brown-skinned legs sticking out of her denim shorts. "And it'll be too cold for wearing shorts. Or for swimming, or soccer, or lots of other stuff. Fall stinks!"

"That's not true! Don't forget all the great stuff about fall," Emily said.

Kara smiled. Emily liked to look on the bright side of everything.

"Like what, Em?" Kara asked.

"Like getting to go back to school," Emily said.

Kara groaned loudly. School definitely wasn't one of her favorite things about fall, or any other time of year. She loved getting to see all her friends every day, and she also loved the chance to get away from her four obnoxious brothers for a while. But other than that, she didn't like much about school.

"It figures Emmers would think of school first," Taylor said with a grin. "After all, her grades are always the best in the class."

Emily blushed. "That's not true." She tugged on a strand of her pale blond hair until it fell over her face. "I got a B minus in gym last year, remember?"

That was Emily. She was shy, and didn't like to brag about anything.

Kara didn't really understand that. If she got almost-straight-As like Emily and Jo did, she would be bragging about it all the time!

"I've got one," Jo said. "In fall the leaves turn pretty colors."

Kara looked around and saw that Jo was right. The big shade trees along Main Street were bright with all the colors of a sunset—orange, red, yellow.

While Kara was looking around at the trees, she spotted Jo's mother walking from the drugstore to the video rental shop next door. Mrs. Sanchez had picked the girls up after school and driven them to the ice-cream parlor. When she finished her shopping, she was going to drive them all home.

Thinking about that reminded Kara of something. "I know another good thing about fall," she said. "Back-to-school shopping! I got lots of good stuff this year."

"Right," Taylor agreed. "And what about Halloween? That's one of the coolest things about fall."

"Ugh," Kara said. "Not when you have four stupid brothers, it isn't. It's their favorite time to try to scare me."

"But what about all that candy?" Jo asked.

Kara took another lick of her ice cream. "Okay, so *that* part of Halloween is pretty cool," she said.

Emily smiled. "See? There are lots of reasons to look forward to fall."

"I've got an idea for another reason," Jo said. "A sleepover!"

"That's an awesome idea," Taylor exclaimed. "We haven't had a sleepover in ages!"

"I call it this time!" Kara cried, jumping up from her seat. She was so excited that she almost dropped her ice-cream cone. "It's my turn to have the sleepover at my house!"

"Cool," Taylor said. "How about doing it this Saturday?"

Jo nodded. "Today is only Tuesday," she said. "That should give us plenty of time to plan. I'll go ask my mom right now if I can go. Hold my ice cream for a second, okay?"

Kara watched as Jo handed her ice-cream cone to Emily and then hurried toward the video store. She wished her mother was there too. She could hardly wait to ask her parents about the party. Kara, Jo, Taylor, and Emily had formed the Sleepover Squad a few months earlier, but they hadn't held a slumber party at Kara's house yet.

"This is going to be great," Kara said. "We can make popcorn, and rent movies, and tell stories till after midnight. . . ."

Just then, Taylor pointed to Kara's arm. "Uh-oh," she said. "Looks like you have a few extra freckles."

Kara looked down. She had been so

busy talking about the sleepover that she'd forgotten to keep eating. A few drops of chocolate ice cream had melted and dripped down onto her arm.

"No problem," she said. She switched her cone to her other hand, then licked the ice-cream drops off her arm. "Now hurry up and eat, everybody. I need to get home and start planning the sleepover!"

"I'm home!" Kara shouted as she burst into her house a few minutes later.

Her second-oldest brother, Eddie, was just coming down the stairs. Eddie was thirteen and thought he was much cooler than Kara.

"Big deal," he said. "Are we supposed to throw a party or something?"

Kara ignored him. She was too excited to let her brother's teasing bother her. She was glad she lived only a few blocks from the ice-cream parlor. That meant Mrs. Sanchez had dropped her off first. And *that* meant she wouldn't have to wait any longer to ask her parents about the sleepover.

She headed straight toward the phone on the little table in the front room. Both her parents worked as engineers, and they usually didn't get home until dinnertime. Up until this year, one of Kara's aunts or older cousins had come over every day to babysit. But now that Chip was fifteen, her parents had decided he was old enough to watch the four younger kids after school.

Kara dialed her mother's office number. "Hi, Mom?" she said when her mother picked up. "It's me. . . ."

She quickly explained about the sleepover. Then she held her breath while she waited for her mother's answer.

"I suppose that would be all right," Mrs. Wyatt said. "I'll call your friends' parents and let them know the party is on."

"Yay!" Kara cheered. "Thanks a million, Mom!"

She said good-bye and hung up. Then she danced across the front room and into the big eat-in kitchen. All four of her brothers were sitting at the table. Six-year-old twins Mark and Todd were reading comic books and eating cheese sticks. Chip was kicking a soccer ball back and forth between his feet. Eddie was drinking a glass of orange juice.

"Hi, Kara," Chip said. "Will you get me a cookie from the cookie jar?"

Normally Kara would have said "Get it yourself." But she was in such a good mood that she smiled at her older brother.

"Sure," she said. "As long as I can get one for myself, too."

"Go for it," Chip said. "There are plenty in there."

Kara spun and twirled her way over to the cookie jar on the counter near the oven. "I hope Mom has time to make more cookies before this weekend," she mumbled to herself. Her mother wasn't as good a cook as Emily's dad or Taylor's housekeeper, but everyone loved her chocolate chip oatmeal cookies.

Kara took the lid off the cookie jar and reached inside. But instead of large squishy-soft cookies, she felt something small and hard. With a frown she pulled out her hand.

"Hey," she said. "What's this?"

In her hand were several hard brown lumps. They looked—and smelled—kind of familiar.

"They're cookies," Todd said with a giggle. "Go ahead and eat one."

Mark was giggling too. "Yeah, it's a new kind Mom bought at the grocery store," he said. "They're delicious!"

Just then the family's dog, a pudgy Labrador retriever named Chester, wandered into the kitchen. As soon as he got near Kara, his nose wriggled and his tail started wagging faster.

That was when Kara figured out what was going on. "These aren't cookies," she exclaimed. "They're some of Chester's dog kibble!"

All four boys burst out laughing. "Rats!" Todd cried. "She figured it out!"

"I thought she was going to eat one!" Mark said.

"Yeah, usually she'll eat anything," Eddie added.

Kara felt her face turning red. She tossed the kibble onto the floor. Chester quickly gobbled it up.

"I'm telling Mom," Kara said. She spun around and headed for the kitchen phone.

"Oh, come on," Chip said with a frown. "Can't you take a joke?"

"You *are* a joke," Kara snapped back. She picked up the phone.

"Not so fast, tattletale," Eddie said before she could dial. "I heard you talking to Mom on the phone just now." He

smirked at the other boys. “She’s having her little friends over on Saturday for one of their stupid girly slumber parties.”

“Ew!” Todd cried.

But Chip was smiling again. “Really?” he said. “In that case, Kara, you’d better not tattle on us. Otherwise, we might decide to do something just as funny during your stupid party.”

Kara gasped. “No way!” she cried,

quickly hanging up the phone. "You can't ruin my sleepover! Swear you won't, and I won't tell Mom about the cookie thing, okay?"

"Hmm." Eddie grinned at Chip. "She sounds kind of nervous, doesn't she?"

Kara gulped. She realized she'd just made a huge mistake.

I forgot the first rule of dealing with brothers, she thought. *Never show weakness!*

But it was too late. "She *does* sound nervous," Chip said. He kicked his soccer ball into the corner and leaned back in his chair. "And she should. Because I just had a great idea."

"What?" Mark asked eagerly.

Kara scowled. "What?" she echoed.

Chip crossed his arms over his chest. "You have to do everything we say between now and Saturday," he said. "Every. Single. Thing. Otherwise, we'll ruin your sleepover."

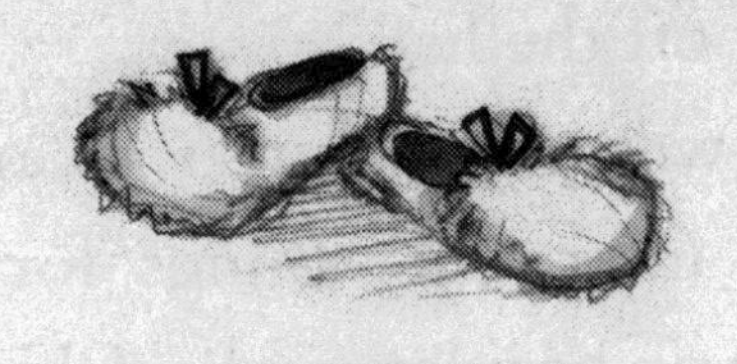

2

A Bad Deal

"Are you crazy?" Kara shrieked, so loudly that Chester ran out of the room with his tail between his legs. "There's no way I'm going to be your stupid servant for the next three days!"

"Three and a half," Eddie corrected.

"Yeah, three and a half," Todd agreed. "Can't you add, Kara?"

Mark laughed loudly. "You'd better not make her do your math homework, Eddie. She got a C in math last year, remember?"

"Good point, squirt," Eddie said. "I'll cross that off the list."

"Don't worry. I'm sure we can think of plenty of interesting things for our new servant to do besides math." Chip grinned. "So, Kara, do we have a deal?"

"Get real!" Kara glared at all four of them. "I'm not doing anything you jerks say. I'm calling Mom right now to tell her about this."

She picked up the phone again.

"Okay." Chip shrugged. "But don't say we didn't warn you."

Kara hesitated. She was so furious with her brothers that all she wanted to do was get them in trouble.

But a little voice in her head was telling her to take a deep breath and think about it. The little voice sounded a lot like Jo. That was probably because it was just the kind of thing Jo would say.

So Kara thought about it. She thought about the time her brothers had put frogs in her lunch box. And the time they'd dyed Chester purple. And the time they'd put toothpaste in Kara's shampoo bottle, and shampoo in her toothpaste tube.

Her brothers didn't let anything stand in their way when they were playing pranks. Not even their parents. Even if Kara tattled, she knew they would find a way to carry out their threat.

She hated feeling so helpless. Usually she wasn't afraid to fight back against whatever her brothers dished out. But this was different. She couldn't let them ruin her sleepover. What if her friends never wanted to come to her house again? It could ruin the whole Sleepover Squad!

When she thought about that, Kara felt like bursting into tears. She wanted to stand up to her brothers, but she couldn't. Not without putting the Sleepover Squad at risk.

That meant she had no choice. She hung up the phone.

"Okay," she said. "I won't call Mom."

"And we have a deal?" Eddie said.

Kara scowled. "It's a deal."

"Good," Chip said. "In that case we can get started right now. I'd like a grape, please. Go get me one."

Kara stomped over to the refrigerator. She yanked open the door and grabbed the bowl of green grapes from the shelf inside.

"Here you go," she said. She dropped the bowl of grapes onto the table.

Eddie reached for the grapes. But Chip stopped him.

"Hold it," he said. "I didn't ask for *grapes*. I asked for *a* grape."

Kara blinked at him. "Huh?"

"I want *one* grape," Chip said. "Not a whole bunch of grapes. Try again."

"Give me a break," Kara muttered. She pulled one grape off the bunch and dropped it onto the table in front of Chip. "There you go. *One* grape. Happy now?"

"Not really." Chip picked up the grape and stared at it. "Those other grapes are in my way."

Without a word Kara grabbed the bowl. She returned it to the refrigerator and shut the door.

When she turned around, she saw Chip popping the grape into his mouth.

"Mmm." He smacked his lips. "That was tasty. Servant, I think I'd like another grape."

Kara glared at him. She could already see where this was going.

She opened the refrigerator and reached inside. She wished she could take the whole bunch of grapes and throw it at her brother's head. Instead, she plucked another grape off the bunch and walked over to the table.

"There you go," she said. "Another grape."

"That looks good," Eddie spoke up. "Servant, I think I'd like a grape too."

Mark and Todd giggled as Kara marched back to the refrigerator. When she returned with Eddie's grape, Mark raised his hand.

"Hey, servant," he said.

"Don't tell me," Kara snapped. "You want a grape, right?"

Mark shook his head. "Nope," he said. "I just remembered something. When I walked Chester after school, he pooped right in front of Mom's rosebushes, and I forgot to clean it up."

"Forgot? Yeah, right." Kara rolled her eyes. Mark and Todd were always getting in trouble for "forgetting" to clean up after the dog.

"Aha!" Eddie said. "That sounds like a job for our servant."

"Yeah," Todd said. "Servant Kara, go pick up that dog doo-doo."

"No way," Kara said. "It was Mark's

turn to walk him. It's his job to clean up after him."

Chip waggled one finger at her. "Are you going back on our deal?"

Kara's shoulders slumped. "No," she mumbled. "I'll go pick it up."

By the time she got back inside after cleaning up after the dog, the boys had disappeared from the kitchen. For a second Kara was relieved.

Maybe they got bored and wandered off, she thought. *After all, Mom's always talking about their short attention spans.*

But a second later the four boys rushed back into the kitchen.

"Oh, there you are, servant," Chip said. "It's about time you got back. We were waiting for you to clean up the table and then serve us our next course."

"Yeah," Mark said. "Goldfish crackers!"

"One at a time," Todd added.

Eddie grinned. "And when you're finished with that, I need you to wash my lucky gym socks. By hand, of course."

Kara sighed loudly. "Stupid dummies," she muttered.

"What was that?" Chip asked. "I thought I heard someone trying to back out of our deal."

"You should get your hearing checked," Kara snapped.

She could tell it was going to be a long three and a half days. *Oh well,* she thought as she started cleaning up the kitchen table. *At least I can spend my spare time thinking up ways to get my revenge once the sleepover is finished. . . .*

3

Twin Trouble

The next day at school Kara was so tired she could hardly keep her eyes open. Her brothers had kept her up very late. They never seemed to run out of ideas for things they could order her to do. First she had to wash all their stinky gym socks by hand. Then they made her clean out under their beds and organize their closets. Her parents gave her a suspicious look when they caught her vacuuming Chip and Eddie's room. But they didn't ask too many questions.

When nine o'clock came, Kara thought she was finally safe. That was her weekday bedtime.

But Chip and Eddie sneaked in at eleven o'clock, after their parents were asleep, and woke Kara up again. They made her fix them a snack, then clean the mud off the bottoms of all their sneakers with an old toothbrush. She wasn't allowed to go back to bed until she'd cleaned out Eddie's pet lizards' cage. He hadn't cleaned it in more than a week, so it took a long time.

When her father came in to wake her for breakfast, Kara felt as if she'd been in bed for only five minutes. She almost fell asleep in her cereal two or three times, and her feet dragged during the whole walk to school.

All morning she did her best to keep her eyes open in class. It was a relief when recess came. She was pretty sure she wouldn't get in trouble for falling asleep during recess.

Kara followed her friends out to the playground. It was another beautiful autumn day. The sun was shining, and the air was crisp. It had rained the night before, and sunlight sparkled off the puddles on the blacktop. All over the playground, kids were running and playing and laughing.

But all Kara wanted to do was curl up in a ball and go to sleep.

"Want to play hopscotch?" Jo asked the others.

Kara yawned. "Maybe later," she mumbled. "Let's go on the swings first."

Sitting on a swing sounded a lot less tiring than playing hopscotch. Kara was trying not to let her friends see that anything was wrong. She didn't want them to know about her deal with her brothers. If they thought the boys might ruin the sleepover, they might not want to come.

Besides, it was kind of embarrassing. Why did she have to be the only one stuck with obnoxious brothers?

Taylor made a face. "We went on the swings yesterday," she said. "Let's do something more exciting."

"We could play jump rope," Emily said. "Does that sound okay, Kara?"

"Whatever," Kara snapped. "If you guys want to play jump rope, let's play jump rope."

She stomped off toward the equipment bins at the edge of the playground. That was where the jump ropes, balls, and other equipment was kept. She was so upset that she stomped right through a puddle and got her sneakers all wet.

Jo caught up to her a second later. "Hey," she said. "Are you okay? You've been acting weird all day."

Kara bit her lip. She should have known

Jo would notice that something was wrong. Jo noticed everything.

"It's nothing," Kara said. "Forget about it. Come on, we'd better go grab a jump rope before they're all taken."

She hurried off again. When she looked over her shoulder, she saw all three of her best friends trading a worried glance.

This time Taylor was the first one to catch up. "Yo, K," she said. "What's your deal today? No offense, but you're acting awfully cranky."

"Yeah," Emily added softly. "That's not like you, Kara. Is something wrong?"

"If there's something wrong, we should talk about it," Jo said. "Or are you not feeling well? Maybe you should go see the school nurse."

Taylor's eyes widened. "Ooh, I didn't even think of that," she said. "When I'm getting sick, I'm always totally cranky."

"Would you guys quit bugging me?"

Kara cried. "I'm not getting sick, okay? And there's nothing I want to talk about either. Isn't anyone allowed to just be tired around here?"

Her friends looked surprised at her outburst. Emily's blue eyes welled up with tears. She was sensitive that way.

Kara felt bad. She hated when Emily got upset.

"Excuse me," Kara mumbled. "I have to go to the bathroom."

She ran off before her friends could say anything. The playground monitor gave her a hall pass, and Kara went back inside.

The school hallway was quiet and echoey. All the students were either outside or sitting in class. Kara walked as slowly as she could toward the bathroom. Her damp sneakers made squeaking sounds against the tile floor.

She didn't really have to use the bathroom. So she just washed her hands instead, then dried them carefully. After that she took off her sneakers and held them under the hand dryer for a while.

Then she put her sneakers back on and just stood there staring at herself in the mirror. Her hazel eyes looked droopy and tired. Her skin looked pale, which made her freckles stand out more than normal. Even her red hair looked less springy than usual.

If she was this tired now, how was she going to survive two and a half more days of being her brothers' servant? Maybe it wasn't worth it.

Then she started imagining some of the things the boys could do to ruin her fun on Saturday. She shuddered. Being their servant was *definitely* worth it. She had to save the sleepover.

She stayed in the bathroom as long as she could. Finally, a fourth grader came in, and Kara decided it was time to leave.

She went back out to the playground. Her friends were watching some other girls play hopscotch.

"What took you so long?" Taylor asked. "We thought you fell in."

Emily peered at her, looking worried. "Are you sure you're not sick?"

Before Kara could answer, she heard shrieks and squeals from nearby. The first graders were pouring out onto the playground. Their recess started a few minutes before the second and third graders went back in.

"Kara! Kara!"

Kara winced. The twins were running toward her, shouting her name. Usually they pretended they didn't even know her. Kara liked it that way.

"Hi there, Carrottop Twins," Taylor greeted the boys. That was her favorite nickname for Mark and Todd. "What's up?"

"We want to go on the seesaw," Todd announced. "But first we want Kara to go clean off the seats with her shirt, in case they're dirty."

Taylor laughed. "Fat chance, Freckle Face," she said.

But Kara was already walking toward

the seesaw. "I'll wipe it off," she grumbled. "But I'm using my pant leg. This is a brand-new shirt."

"Whatever," Mark said. "Just hurry up."

Kara scowled at him. She wasn't happy that the twins were ordering her around in front of her friends. But if she didn't do as they said, they would tell Chip and Eddie. And then she could forget about having a fun sleepover.

Only one seesaw was free. Kara kneeled on one seat, rubbing it with the knees of her jeans. Then she did the other seat. She tried not to look at her friends. They were standing nearby, watching her.

The twins were watching too. "Okay, that's clean enough," Todd said. "But don't go anywhere. We might need you for something else."

"Yeah." Mark sat down on the low end of the seesaw. Then he looked down at his sneaker. "Hey, my shoe is untied. Come over here and tie it."

Kara clenched her fists. She wanted to rip Mark's shoe off and bonk him over the head with it. Instead, she forced herself to smile.

"Okay," she said. "Hold still. . . ."

She bent down and tied her brother's sneaker. Out of the corner of her eye, she could see her friends. They all looked astonished.

Just then the bell rang. That meant it was time for the older kids to go back inside.

"Oops," Kara said. "I have to go."

She hurried away before the boys could say anything. Her friends caught up with her halfway to the school door.

"Okay, what was that all about?" Taylor demanded.

Kara felt her face turn red. "Nothing," she mumbled.

But she knew it was no use playing dumb. Her friends weren't stupid. They could see that something strange was going on.

"Kara . . . ," Emily began softly.

Kara didn't even wait for her to finish. "Okay, okay!" she cried, throwing her hands into the air. "I might as well tell you. But you're not going to like it."

She quickly told them the whole story. By the time she'd finished, all three of her friends looked horrified and outraged.

"I can't believe they're doing this!" Emily exclaimed.

"Yeah." Jo shook her head. "That's pretty obnoxious, even for your brothers, Kara."

"You can't let them get away with this, K," Taylor declared.

Kara shrugged. "What else can I do?" she said. "If I don't go along with their stupid deal, they'll play practical jokes on us and be total jerks during our sleep-over."

Taylor smiled. "So what?" she said. "How bad can it be? If they want to play that game, tell them to bring it on!"

4

Enough Is Enough!

By the time school ended, Kara still wasn't sure what to think. Part of her agreed with Taylor. Maybe the best thing to do was plan their own prank to get back at the boys. That might teach them a lesson.

But another part of her was nervous. Taylor and the others didn't know just how obnoxious Kara's brothers could be.

"You guys don't understand," she told them when they were all walking out of the school building. "None of you knows what it's like to have brothers."

"I do," Jo said.

Kara had almost forgotten about Jo's brother, Alfonso. He was so much older that he seemed more like an uncle or cousin than a brother. Besides, he wasn't even around that much anymore. He and Jo's sister, Lydia, were both in college. That meant they lived in a different state for most of the year.

"Al doesn't count," Kara said. "He's not an immature dodo-head like my brothers." She took a deep breath. "Anyway, it doesn't matter. I can go along with their stupid deal for a few more days if it means saving the sleepover."

"Are you sure?" Emily looked doubtful.

Kara *wasn't* sure. She wasn't very good at going along with things she didn't like. And she definitely didn't like being her brothers' servant.

But she nodded. "I can do it," she said. "I *have* to. Besides, maybe my parents will catch them bossing me around. If they figure out what's going on, they might send all four of them to reform school before this weekend."

Her friends laughed. "That would be nice," Jo said. "But don't worry, Kara. Things will be okay either way."

"That's right," Taylor agreed. "If you have to break the deal and the boys go ahead with their threats, we're up for the challenge."

Emily nodded. "How bad could it be?"

"Bad." Kara shuddered. "Don't you remember the time they locked me in the basement and told the babysitter I ran away? Or the time they tricked me into eating a worm sandwich?"

Taylor waved one hand in the air. "Those pranks were totally lame," she said. "I'm sure we could come up with something much more creative."

"But only if we have to," Emily put in. She sounded kind of worried.

"Only if we have to," Jo agreed.

Taylor shrugged. "Sure," she said. "But if we have to, we have to. And those boys will be sorry they messed with us."

She didn't sound very worried at all. That made Kara feel a little bit better.

They were outside the school by now. Emily looked over at the curb where parents could pull up in their cars.

"There's my dad," she said. Emily's father was a teacher at the high school. He picked her up from school every day after he finished grading papers.

"I'd better go get on my bus," Jo said. "Good luck, Kara."

"Thanks. I'll need it." Kara waved as Emily and Jo hurried off in opposite directions.

"Ready to go?" Taylor asked.

Taylor and Kara both walked home from

school. Kara's house was just five blocks away, and Taylor's was a few blocks farther.

They joined a bunch of kids waiting on the curb. When the crossing guard waved them on, they all crossed the street.

"So what are we going to do at our sleepover?" Taylor asked. "Do you have lots of ideas?"

"Well, not *lots*," Kara said. She jumped over a puddle on the sidewalk. "I've been so busy doing everything my brothers say that I've barely had time to think about it. But Mom and Dad said they would rent us some movies, and—"

"Kara! Kara!"

It was the twins. They walked home from school too. Just like on the playground, they usually ignored her and walked with their own friends. But not today.

"What do you want?" Kara asked.

Mark and Todd grinned. "We want that big yellow leaf over there in the gutter,"

Mark said. "Go get it for us, servant Kara."

"You guys are really obnoxious, did you know that?" Kara grumbled. "I can't believe I'm related to you. Mom and Dad won't admit it, but I bet I'm adopted."

Taylor laughed. "I don't think so."

Kara knew she was right. All the Wyatt kids looked alike. They all had wavy red hair and lots of freckles.

Kara went over and picked up the yellow leaf. She held it out to the boys.

"Put it in your hair," Mark ordered.

"What?" Kara said.

Mark pointed to her head. "Put it in your hair. You know—like a decoration."

Kara looked around. All the other kids were at least half a block ahead of them. Nobody was looking at her except Taylor and the twins.

I have to save the sleepover, she thought.

Reaching up, she stuck the yellow leaf

into her thick red hair. Mark pointed and laughed.

"Kara's a tree!" he cried.

Meanwhile Todd pulled a granola bar out of his pocket. He held it out to Kara.

"Hey, servant Kara, open this for me," he said.

Kara grabbed the granola bar. "Do you want me to eat it for you too, you little twerp?"

"It's okay," Taylor whispered. "If you can't take it anymore, just quit. We can handle it."

"No." Hearing Taylor say that made Kara feel stronger. "It's okay." She unwrapped the granola bar and handed it back to Todd. "Here you go. Be careful not to choke on it."

For the next couple of blocks the twins continued to order Kara around. Taylor tried to help with some of the ridiculous tasks, but the boys wouldn't let her. They wanted Kara to do everything herself.

Another crossing guard waved them across Dogwood Street. "Only two blocks and you'll be home," Taylor whispered to Kara as they hurried across.

Kara shrugged. "Big deal," she said. "Chip and Eddie are there already, remember? That means twice as many jerky brothers to boss me around."

Todd hopped up onto the curb on the other side of the street. There was a big mud puddle at the edge of the sidewalk. Todd reached into his backpack and took out a baseball. He leaned over and dropped it into the puddle. It landed with a splash, sending mud flying everywhere.

"Servant Kara!" he cried. "My baseball fell. Pick it up for me."

Kara leaned over to pick up the wet, muddy baseball. She tried to use only her fingertips. She hated getting dirty. But she wasn't going to let the boys see that it bothered her.

"Here you go," she said, holding out the ball.

Todd wrinkled his nose. "Ew, it's all dirty," he said. "Servant Kara, wipe it off on your shirt."

"No way," Kara said. "I'll wipe it on my

jeans if you want. But I'm not using my new shirt to clean your stupid baseball."

Mark crossed his arms. "Didn't you hear him, servant Kara? He said to use your *shirt*."

"Use your shirt! Use your shirt!" Todd chanted.

Kara looked down at her new shirt. She could feel her face going red. Both boys were chanting now. They were so loud that some of the other kids were looking back at them curiously. Taylor was biting her lip, looking worried.

"Hurry up, servant!" Mark told Kara. "Otherwise we'll have to tell Chip you went back on our deal."

Enough was enough.

"Go ahead and tell him!" Kara yelled. She threw the ball at the boys. "The deal is off!"

5

Breaking the Deal

Kara stomped off toward home. She didn't even stop when Taylor called her name. She was too furious to talk.

But Taylor caught up and grabbed her arm. "Hey, K," Taylor said. "Don't be upset. It'll be okay."

Kara glared at her. "That's easy for you to say," she cried. "You don't have to live with them!"

Just then the twins came running toward them. Kara clenched her fists. If they ordered her to do one more thing, she was going to push *them* into a mud puddle!

But the boys ran right past her. They made a beeline for their house, which was just a block away now.

"See?" Taylor said. "Looks like you scared them. Maybe they'll leave you alone now."

"Yeah, I wish," Kara muttered. "That would only happen in opposite land."

The two girls started walking again. "Look on the bright side," Taylor said. "At least now you don't have to do what they say anymore. You're free!"

"Look on the bright side?" In spite of her bad mood Kara smiled a little. "You sound like Emily."

Taylor laughed. "She must be rubbing off on me."

"Me too," Kara said. "Trying to go along with the boys' stupid deal sounds like something she would do. She always does her best to get along with people." She sighed. "But I should know better. Getting along with my brothers is hopeless."

They were almost to her house by now. Kara stopped on the sidewalk and looked up. Usually she loved coming home. Her house was built of brick, just like most of the others on the block. It wasn't as old as Emily's family's farmhouse, but it was a lot older than the homes in Jo's development. The paint on the shutters was starting to peel, and there were weeds in the flower beds, but the whole place looked happy and lived-in.

The inside was just as well-worn and well-loved as the outside. The rooms weren't as big as the ones in Taylor's house, but the ceilings were high and the windows let in lots of light. Kara's favorite part of the house was her cozy bedroom at the top of the attic stairs. She was the only one in the family who had her own room, since she was the only girl.

But today she dreaded going inside. What would be waiting for her in there?

Taylor smiled at her. "Hang in there," she said. "You only have to put up with them until Saturday. Then they won't have the slumber party to hold over your head anymore."

Kara said good-bye to Taylor and headed for the door. Inside she found all four of her brothers waiting for her in the front room.

"The twins told us what happened." Chip had his arms crossed over his chest. "Would you like to explain yourself, servant?"

"Don't call me that anymore," Kara shot back. "And I don't have to explain anything to you."

Eddie raised his eyebrows. "Did you hear that, Chip?" he said. "Our servant is talking back."

Chip shook his head. "Tsk, tsk," he said. "Now, Kara, I'm going to give you one last chance to apologize for this shocking behavior. Then we can get back to our deal."

Kara scowled. "I'm tired of bringing you snacks and washing your stinky socks. You can do it yourselves from now on."

"Oh yeah?" Mark cried. "You'd better do what we say, or else!"

"Forget it." Kara put her hands on her hips. "The deal is off."

Chip and Eddie traded a glance. "Okay, if that's how you feel about it," Chip said.

Eddie shrugged. "You'll be sorry."

"I'm already sorry," Kara snapped. "Sorry I have brothers!"

For the rest of the afternoon the boys did their best to drive Kara crazy. They whispered to one another whenever she walked by, and made funny faces every time she looked at them.

But that wasn't all. Kara was watching TV in her parents' room when she heard footsteps up on the third floor. She jumped up and ran upstairs.

"Hey, are you guys in my room?" she yelled. "You'd better not be in there!"

But the boys weren't in her room. They were in the other half of the attic. Eddie was carrying a big cardboard box.

"What are you doing?" Kara asked.

"Halloween is coming," Chip said. "So we decided to get out all our old monster masks."

"Halloween is weeks away," Kara said. "Why did you get them out now?"

Eddie set the box down at the top of the steps. "We just want to be prepared."

"Yeah," Mark said with a giggle.

"Prepared for anything," Todd added.

Kara stared at Mark's werewolf mask

lying near the top of the box. Emily was terrified of big, mean dogs. . . .

Later, Kara was coming in from walking Chester when she saw something scuttle under the coffee table in the front room. "Aaaah!" she screamed.

Eddie strolled into the room. "What's wrong?"

"I saw something crawl under there," Kara said. "It looked like . . . Wait a minute."

She bent down and peered under the table. Looking back at her was one of Eddie's pet lizards. When she turned around, she saw Chester sniffing at the second lizard. It was perched on the back of the sofa.

Eddie grinned. "Oh, did Bubba and Clyde startle you?" he said. "Sorry about that. I'm just letting them get some exercise."

Kara glared at him. She was used to the lizards by now. But when Eddie first got them, she had thought they were ugly and kind of scary. How would her friends feel if they saw the lizards walking around the house while they were there?

"I hope you're not planning on exercising them a lot in the next few days," she said. "Like this Saturday, for instance?"

"I don't know what you're talking about," Eddie said with a smirk.

By the time her parents got home, Kara was feeling jumpy and suspicious. Her head was spinning with all the possible pranks her brothers might pull at her sleepover. What if her friends never wanted to sleep over at her house again? What if they decided they didn't even want her in the Sleepover Squad anymore?

I wish I could have kept up that stupid deal, she thought. *I wish I wasn't so worried about what might happen on Saturday night.*

But most of all, I wish I didn't have any brothers!

6

Waiting and Wondering

"You were totally right, Emmers," Taylor said happily. "Fall is great!"

She took a big bite of the doughnut she was holding. Powdered sugar poofed out from the doughnut and onto Taylor's chin.

Kara laughed. "Hey, Taylor, you look like you have a white beard."

It was Saturday, and the four members of the Sleepover Squad were at Thompson Orchards. That was an orchard a few miles from Emily's house. Every autumn it was open to the public for apple picking, hayrides, and other fun fall activities. Emily's father had picked all the girls up and driven them there. In a little while he would drop them off at Kara's house for the sleepover.

"Can we go on the pony rides again?" Emily asked.

"Sure," Taylor said. "I want to ride the spotted one this time."

"A spotted pony is called a pinto," Emily said.

Emily knew a lot about horses. Her bedroom was filled with toy horses and horse books. Kara knew that Emily wanted to take riding lessons more than anything else in the world. But her parents still thought she was too young.

"We still have to try the corn maze, too," Jo said. "It looks like fun."

Emily nodded. "I almost forgot about that," she said. "Should we do that next?"

"Let's finish our doughnuts first, then do the pony rides," Jo said. "We should still have plenty of time for the maze."

Kara nodded along with the others. She was having fun at the orchard. But at the same time, everything they did reminded her of what might be waiting for them when they got back to her house. While they were picking apples, she wondered if the boys were at home hiding rotten bananas in her sleeping bag. When she felt the stiff hay poking her in the legs during the hayride, it reminded her of a lizard's claws walking on her in her sleep. As she took a sip of apple cider, she imagined her brothers pouring salt water or liquid soap into the orange juice carton.

Her friends finished eating. Kara popped the last bite of doughnut into her mouth and wiped the sugar off her fingers. Then she zipped up her jacket a little tighter. It was sunny, but chilly. She jammed her hands into her pockets and followed her friends toward the pony rides.

The sleepover hasn't even started yet, and my brothers are already ruining my fun! she thought, feeling a little grumpy.

When the girls finished their pony rides, Emily's father was waiting for them. "Almost ready to go?" he asked. "I told Kara's parents I'd have you there by three."

"Not yet, Daddy," Emily said. "We didn't go in the corn maze yet."

"Okay." Mr. McDougal smiled. "Go on and do the maze—as long as Kara doesn't mind putting off the start of her sleepover a few more minutes."

"No way," Kara said. "I don't mind at all."

The girls ran over to the corn maze. It was built out of tall cornstalks and straw bales. There was an entrance at one end, and an exit at the other end, with lots of twists and turns and dead ends in between.

Anyone who made it through without help got a free apple.

There were a few other kids in the maze when the girls entered. The girls could hear them laughing and yelling, but they couldn't see them. A few feet from the entrance the path split in two.

"This way," Jo said. She pointed down the right-hand path. "I bet this is the way."

"Only one way to find out!" Taylor grinned and charged down the path. Jo and Emily were right behind her.

Kara trailed behind the others. She was still thinking about her brothers. What were they doing right now?

"Dead end!" Taylor yelled. The girls had just turned a corner and found a wall of straw bales in front of them.

"Oops," Jo said. "Guess my bet was wrong."

"That's okay." Emily smiled and shrugged. "I was going to guess this way too."

Just then Jo looked at Kara. "Hey," she said. "Are you okay? You're being kind of quiet."

Kara didn't want to make her friends nervous about the sleepover. But she couldn't keep her worries to herself for another second.

"It's my stupid brothers," she blurted out.

"I'm sure they're at home right now setting up all kinds of crazy practical jokes!"

Taylor reached out and put an arm around her. "Don't worry," she said. "We'll deal with them later."

"Yeah," Jo added. "Don't let them ruin your fun now."

Kara sighed loudly. "But I can't help it! They could be doing anything."

"So what?" Taylor said. "No matter what lame stuff they do to us, we'll come up with something ten times better to get back at them."

"I guess you're right." Kara forced herself to smile.

But inside she wasn't so sure. What could her nice friends do against the most obnoxious boys in the world?

Half an hour later Mr. McDougal dropped the girls off at the curb in front of Kara's house. "Have fun, kids," he said.

Emily, Taylor, and Jo said good-bye and thanked him for the ride. But Kara was distracted. She'd just spotted her brothers. They were raking leaves in the front yard.

"Just ignore them," Kara whispered to her friends as they started toward the house. "Don't even look at them."

"Hi there, girls!" Chip called loudly as they walked past.

"Hi," Emily called back. Then she smiled sheepishly at Kara. "Sorry," she said. "I was just being polite."

Soon the girls were inside. "Should we watch a movie?" Kara asked. "Mom and Dad rented a bunch for us. We could make microwave popcorn—Mom got the movie-theater-butter kind."

"We can do that when it gets dark," Taylor said. "Maybe we should go outside for a while first." Taylor loved being outside. She got restless if she had to stay inside for too long.

Kara bit her lip. "Outside?" she said. "But my brothers are out there."

Taylor frowned. "Are you going to let those boys stop us from doing what we want?"

"We could do both." Emily held up one of the DVDs. "This one's only half an hour long. We could watch it and still have lots of time to play outside before dinnertime."

"That's a great idea," Jo agreed.

Kara nodded. Maybe by the time the video finished, the boys would have wandered off somewhere.

But the DVD was only half over when she heard the front door bang open. She looked up and saw all four of her brothers walking in. They all paused by the door just long enough to shrug off their jackets and hang them up on the coatrack.

She clutched her popcorn bowl closer. What would they do now? Were they planning to throw leaves in the girls' hair? Or were their pockets full of spiders? Or did they have something even more horrible in mind?

7

Gotcha!

Chip took a step closer. Kara held her breath.

"Excuse me," Chip said. "Can I have a handful of popcorn? Raking is hungry work."

"Sure." Taylor held out the bowl she was sharing with Emily. "Have some of ours."

"Thanks." Chip scooped up some popcorn. Then he glanced around at his brothers. "Come on, guys. Let's go down in the rec room and leave them alone."

"Okay," Eddie said. "I call first turn on the pinball machine."

"No way!" Todd cried. He and Mark raced ahead toward the basement door. A moment later all the boys had disappeared down the stairs.

Kara was so surprised she could hardly talk for a second. "What's going on?" she exclaimed. "Why didn't they do anything obnoxious?"

Jo reached for some popcorn. "Maybe they're afraid they'll get in trouble."

"No way," Kara said. "Mom and Dad are way out in the back watering the garden. This was their perfect chance to get us."

"I know!" Emily's face lit up. "Maybe this *is* their big prank! Maybe their plan is to drive you crazy and make you worry all night while they do nothing."

Kara shrugged. "Maybe," she said. "But I doubt it. My brothers aren't that clever."

The others returned their attention

to the video. But Kara kept staring at the basement door. What were the boys really plotting down there?

"That was great!" Taylor said when the video ended a few minutes later. "Ready to go outside now?"

"Okay," Kara said. "But first maybe we should set up our sleeping area for later."

Even Taylor agreed with that. It was always fun to lay out their sleeping bags and pillows.

Kara led the way up to the second floor, then down the hall toward the attic steps.

Chip and Eddie's bedroom door was closed. But Emily peeked into the twins' room as she passed. "I think you were too worried about your brothers, Kara," she said. "They probably won't do anything that bad tonight."

"Yeah," Taylor said. "They probably realized they shouldn't mess with the

Sleepover Squad, or they'd be sorry."

Kara smiled weakly. She hoped her friends were right. But she still wasn't so sure.

"I hope there's room for all of us on your floor, Kara," Jo said as they started up the narrow steps.

"There is," Kara said. "Mom helped me clean up yesterday. We put some of my projects away for now."

Kara liked to create dioramas, sculpt things out of clay, build model planes and houses, and do all sorts of other art projects. Usually there were at least two or three of her projects spread out on her desk and floor at a time. Since her room wasn't very big, the projects didn't leave much space for anything else.

At the top of the stairs was a tiny landing. Two doors opened off it. One led to the storage part of the attic. The other one opened into Kara's room.

Kara reached for the knob. "Welcome to my . . . ," she began. Then she frowned.

"What's wrong?" Jo asked.

"The doorknob's all slippery." Kara lifted her hand to her nose and sniffed. "Butter!"

She grabbed the knob tighter and opened the door. "Wait!" Taylor yelled from right behind her. "Don't step forward!"

Kara looked down. There were at least a dozen eggs lined up just inside the doorway. If Taylor hadn't stopped her, Kara would have stepped right on one.

She clenched her fists. "I told you guys my brothers were up to no good!" she cried. "Look at poor Chester!"

The dog was sitting in the middle of Kara's bed. The only way to recognize him was by his wagging tail. He was wearing a hideous green and black monster mask that made him look like a creature from another planet.

Emily giggled as she stepped carefully over the eggs. "Um, interesting posters, Kara," she said. "Did you redecorate just for us?"

As Kara looked around, her heart sank. Her cozy little room looked like a different place. The boys had replaced the nice pictures on her walls with their own ugly wrestling posters and photos cut out of magazines—photos of toilets, bugs, and snakes.

"Do you think they messed with our stuff?" Taylor asked, leaping forward toward the pile of suitcases and sleeping bags at the foot of Kara's bed. Mr. McDougal had dropped off their things on the way to the orchard.

"I don't know," Kara said grimly. "But be careful."

Jo zipped open her suitcase and made a face. "Ugh," she said. "There are worms in my bag!"

"Ew!" Taylor cried, leaning over to look.

"Don't squish them," Emily said. "Worms are good. I'll help you get them out in a second. Then we can put them in the flower beds outside."

She and Taylor each unzipped their bags.

"No way!" Taylor shrieked. "Those dorks put a bunch of stinky socks in here. All my stuff is going to smell!"

"They took everything out of mine and filled it with rocks," Emily said. "Where are my pajamas?"

Kara sat down on the edge of her bed. She put her head in her hands. This was even worse than she'd feared.

Just then she heard a giggle from the doorway. She looked up and saw Mark's face peeking in. A second later Eddie appeared behind him. He was grinning.

"You jerks!" Kara screamed. "I'll get you for this!"

She leaped up and raced for the door.

Her heart was pounding, and her head was throbbing with rage. She was ready to strangle all four boys with her bare hands.

Taylor caught her by the arm. "Wait!" she said. "Kara, calm down a second."

"How can I calm down?" Kara was so furious that there were tears in her eyes. She waved a hand at the chaos around her. "Look at what they did!"

She wriggled to get away. But Taylor grabbed her by both shoulders. She was taller and stronger than Kara, so Kara had to stop.

"Hold on," Taylor said quietly. "Listen to me, Kara. There's a better way to get back at them. . . ."

8

Get Mad or Get Even?

For a few minutes Kara didn't want to listen to Taylor. All she wanted was to pound her brothers. Or maybe just dunk their heads in the toilet until they begged for mercy.

"You guys better run!" she screamed when she heard them racing off down the steps. "You better run all the way to Timbuktu if you don't want me to kill you!"

She tried to break free of Taylor's grip. But Jo stepped forward to help Taylor.

"Settle down, Kara," Jo said. "Going loco won't fix anything. It's exactly what they want."

"Let me go," Kara cried. "If you don't want me to kill them, at least let me go get Mom and Dad. When they see this mess, *they'll* kill them!"

"You don't need to tattle," Taylor said. "That will only make things worse."

"What are you talking about?" Kara cried. "How could things get worse? They ruined our sleepover!"

Emily put a hand on her arm. "No, they didn't."

Kara blinked. Suddenly she realized something. Her friends didn't look nearly as upset as she was. If she didn't know better, she might even think they were having . . . fun. None of them were crying or calling their parents to pick them up.

"I don't get it," she said. "Aren't you guys mad about this?"

"Well, I'm not exactly thrilled about cleaning worms out of my underwear," Jo said with a laugh. "But we all figured your brothers would make trouble."

"Yeah," Emily said. "Sort of the way we figured the sun would set tonight and rise again in the morning."

Taylor and Jo giggled. "No," Taylor said. "We were *more* sure about her brothers than we were about the sun."

Kara stared at them. Then she looked around her room. She couldn't believe it. Her friends didn't even have obnoxious brothers. They weren't used to these sorts of pranks.

"So you aren't so upset that you never want to come over again?" she asked.

"Don't be silly," Jo said. "It's not that big a deal."

Emily nodded. "The only thing we're upset about is that *you're* so upset."

"Yeah." Taylor grinned. "And don't

worry, we're going to make them pay for that!"

"Do you want a tissue?" Emily asked Kara. "I have some in the outside pocket of my suitcase . . . or at least I did. There might be rocks in there now. But I can check."

"Thanks." Kara sniffled. She realized that tears had been streaming down her face while she screamed at her brothers.

Emily reached for her bag. There was a big pocket on the outside. When she unzipped the flap, something inside the pocket moved.

"Eep!" Emily squeaked, jumping back quickly.

A second later a small, scaly green head popped out and looked around. It was one of Eddie's lizards.

Kara sighed. "Sorry, Em."

Emily swallowed hard. "It's—it's okay," she said. "Um, can one of you help me get it out of there, though?"

A little while later Kara raced down the basement steps. Her brothers were in the rec room. Chip and Eddie were playing air hockey. The twins were sprawled on the beat-up brown sofas reading comic books.

"Hey, look who's here," Eddie said when he spotted Kara. "How did you like our decorating job in your room?"

"Yeah, how many eggs did you step on, Kara?" Mark asked.

"Did you find the worms?" Todd added. "That was my idea."

"Never mind all that!" Kara cried, her eyes wide. She waved her hands to shut them up. "Listen, this is serious!"

"What?" Chip looked suspicious.

"It's Emily!" A few tears squeezed out of the corners of Kara's eyes. "When she found Bubba in her suitcase, she got really upset and ran outside crying."

"It was Clyde, not Bubba," Eddie corrected. "Bubba is in your sock drawer."

"She really ran out like that?" Chip looked sort of guilty, but then he shrugged. "Well, so what? We can't help it if your friend is a big wimp, just like you."

"No, no, that's not the problem," Kara cried. "When she ran out, she left the front door open behind her, and Chester got out and ran off down the street. Now he's missing!"

9

The Last Laugh

"No way!" Chip sounded panicky. "Come on, guys. We've got to find Chester!"

They raced up the stairs. Kara hurried after them. She reached the front room just in time to see the boys grab their jackets from the coatrack by the door. They ran out without another word, slamming the door behind them.

Kara turned and walked around the couch. Her friends were kneeling behind it.

"You can come out now," Kara said. "They're gone."

"We heard." Taylor stood up and grinned. "We could hear you all the way in the basement too."

Emily nodded. "You're a great actress, Kara," she said. "If I didn't know better, I would have thought you were really upset."

Kara giggled. "Thanks. Where's Chester?"

"We shut him in your parents' room so he wouldn't bark when the boys ran out," Jo said. "I'll go let him out now."

"Yeah," Taylor said. "He won't want to miss what happens next!"

Soon Jo returned with Chester. Kara walked over and grabbed his leash from the coatrack.

"Let's go out on the porch and wait," she suggested. "Chester can sit with us."

"Good idea," Taylor said.

Soon the four girls were sitting on the front porch. Kara and Jo were on the swing. Emily was sitting on the floor scratching Chester's ears. Even though she was afraid of most big dogs, she liked Chester. He was too lazy and gentle to be scary.

Taylor was pacing back and forth at the top of the porch steps. "It sounds like a lot of kids are still outside playing," she said. "That's good."

Kara nodded. It was still a little before dinnertime. A lot of people in the neighborhood were outside enjoying the nice autumn afternoon. A group of teenagers was shooting baskets in the Farleys' driveway two doors down, and some younger kids were jumping in leaf piles in one of the yards across the street. The sounds of kids talking and playing came from every direction.

And soon, another sound came from

every direction. "Listen," Taylor said. "I think it's working."

There was a loud shriek of laughter from down the block. Then another, and another.

Soon, all that the girls could hear was laughing. A moment later Kara's parents appeared from around the corner of the house. Mrs. Wyatt was wearing gardening gloves, and Mr. Wyatt had the newspaper tucked under one arm.

"What's going on out there?" Mr. Wyatt asked the girls. "We were in the backyard, and we heard all the racket."

"I don't know, Dad," Kara said with a grin. "Sounds like something funny is happening out there."

Her friends all burst out laughing. Mr. and Mrs. Wyatt looked suspicious. They traded a curious glance.

Before they could ask any more questions, there was another shout of laughter.

This time it came from the basketball players. A moment later Chip, Eddie, Mark, and Todd raced toward the porch.

"Hi, boys!" Taylor called loudly, waving to them. "Look, we found Chester."

Chester barked and wagged his tail.

Chip leaped up onto the porch and glared at the girls. He was red-faced and out of breath, just like the other boys. They were all carrying their jackets bundled up in their arms.

"You guys did this, didn't you?" Chip cried. "Stupid jerks!"

"Hold on there, champ," Mr. Wyatt said sternly. "Don't yell at your sister and her friends."

"But look what they did!" Eddie held up his jacket.

Kara put a hand over her mouth to hold back her giggles. A big sign was pinned to the back of Eddie's jacket with at least a dozen safety pins. It said I PICK MY NOSE.

Chip, Mark, and Todd held up their jackets too. All of them had similar signs. Chip's said I'M AFRAID OF GIRLS. Mark's said I HAVE COOTIES. Todd's said I EAT DOG POOP.

"Everyone in the neighborhood saw us walking around like this!" Eddie exclaimed. He sounded outraged.

"*They* did it!" Todd pointed to Kara and the other girls.

"Yeah," Chip said. "They knew we'd rush out so fast we wouldn't notice until it was too late."

Mark scowled and tried to rip his sign off his jacket. "You guys are in big trouble now," he said. "We caught you red-handed."

For a second Kara was worried. What if her parents took the boys' side?

"I see," her father said slowly. He glanced over at his wife. "And just why were you rushing out so fast, boys?"

"We thought Chester ran away," Todd said.

"And why would you think that?" Mrs. Wyatt asked. "He's sitting right here."

"Yeah, but Kara told us Emily let him out," Eddie said.

"That doesn't sound like something Emily would do," his father said. "She's a very careful and responsible girl."

Emily blushed. "Thank you, Mr. Wyatt."

"Ask them why they thought Em let him out," Kara said.

"Good question," Mr. Wyatt said. "Boys?"

Since Mr. and Mrs. Wyatt were both engineers, that meant they were very logical people. Jo was a logical person too. She was the one who had said Kara's parents would figure out what had really happened. And she was right. A few minutes later Kara's parents had the whole story.

"Okay, so maybe we played a few pranks," Eddie said with a frown. "But their prank was just mean!"

"Maybe a little." Mrs. Wyatt looked as if she were trying not to laugh. "But somehow I doubt they would have done it if you hadn't played all those jokes on them first."

"Yes," Mr. Wyatt added. "I think we can call this one a draw." He smiled. "Although, boys, you really ought to be ashamed of yourselves. The girls' prank was much more clever than yours."

"Thanks, Dad," Kara said.

"You're welcome." Her father winked at her. "But that doesn't mean I want to encourage this sort of thing in the future."

"Don't worry, Mr. W," Taylor said. "We won't be playing any more pranks. Unless absolutely necessary, that is." She turned and grinned at the boys.

They scowled back at her. "Whatever," Chip muttered. "Can we go inside now?"

Kara laughed as they slunk away. She was pretty sure the kids in the neighborhood would be talking about this prank for a long time. She was also pretty sure that she and her friends would be able to enjoy the rest of the sleepover without any further mischief from her brothers.

At least *this* time . . .

Slumber Party Project: Joking Around

Some pranks are mean, but some can be fun. Try these tricks to liven up your next sleepover.

1. Icky Ice: Buy some fake bugs or other creepy crawlies at the toy store or dollar store. Get an adult to help you freeze them into ice cubes. Then serve them to your friends and wait for the screams!

2. Slippery Sink: Put petroleum jelly or butter on the handles of the bathroom sinks—right before it's time for your

friends to brush their teeth. Then stand back and laugh when they try to turn on the water!

3. Rainbow Milk: Ask your parents to buy milk in a cardboard carton (not a see-through jug). Put a few drops of food coloring in the milk (red, green, or blue work well). Then serve your friends cereal for breakfast, and watch their faces when they pour in the colorful milk!